AF444571

"Nuh ebery ting dat ave sugar,

sweet"

Jamaican proverb.

Book One: Vodún Heirloom.

Prologue:

22 November 1718

Ocracoke, Province of North Carolina.

Jack leaped out of bed to the loud bangs and echoing thunder of cannon fire. Unsure of what the obtrusive noise was, he nevertheless knew that something was badly wrong. He wrestled Juliette and his four-year-old daughter Josephine out of their deep slumber and informed them of the situation. Lacking details, he engendered more questions than he could answer.

"This is no time for speculation," Jack said. He told his wife and daughter to lay low and hide if necessary while he went out to investigate. He then ran to the closet and retrieved his two Queen Anne flintlock pistols, replacements for the two lost at the fat man's plantation when he rescued his wife from damnation. He primed, powdered and loaded both pistols, using the ramrod to secure the ball and wad. Afterward, he handed one of the pistols off to Juliette with an unspoken understanding of the potential danger.

Above the front door in its sheath was his rapier. He retrieved it and exited through the door, slamming it shut behind him. He waited for the sound of his wife to latch the lock before moving on.

Stealthy he made his way to the Adventure, a sloop that

served as the last of Blackbeard's Armada.

The Adventure was about 65 feet in length and weighed 80 tons. She was built in Jamaica. She had one raked mast with a main topsail, two jibs and a gaff rigged mainsail. The Adventure could house 10-12 cannons. Compared to the abandoned flagship of Blackbeard's Armada, the Queen Anne's Revenge, which boasted 40 canons, the Adventure came up short. Albeit they had less firepower, the men under Blackbeard's command were fierce and knew how to pack a punch.

Jack came up to the Adventure and climbed up a rope ladder on the aft, starboard side. He eased himself over the railing and onto the deck hiding behind a coil of large hemp rope. Spotting Edward Teach and Edward's men yelling exchanges with British sailors, he hastily made his way towards them.

"Damnation, seize my soul if I give you quarters, or take any from you," Jack heard his cousin, Teach, better known as Blackbeard, yell at what he would later learn were English sailors led by lieutenant Robert Maynard and commissioned by the governor of Virginia.

Having lost the element of surprise the English sailors were sitting ducks.

The Adventure, freed from her anchorage by its men, quickly maneuvered itself into a position to fire on the two British Navy shallow draft bottom boats, the Ranger and the Jane, beached on sand rails.

Jack was wide-eyed, open-mouthed and awestruck at the sights and sounds playing out before him. The Adventure tore the Ranger to pieces and scattered the men of the Jane.

"Jackson, it's good to see you again man! I feared I was not to see you as we made good our escape. Where is Juliette and Josephine?" Edward asked crisply but compassionately.

"They are safe, back at our dwelling. We are to meet at a rendezvous point if I'm not back relatively soon. What's the plan?" Jack asked.

"Jackson, always loyal to a fault, if all of my men had half of your loyalty I probably would have had to pay them twice the booty. Thank the Gods my men are a bunch of degenerates.

"The men and I are going to sack that puny little vessel and show these lily livered cravins a lesson on civility. Scallywags! They dare to sneak up on me in the middle of the night like coward hyena's. Once we settle this skirmish then it's off to French Louisiana my good man!

"We shall sail to the New Orleans territory and from there navigate her bayous and find new dwellings for us all. It's ripe with potential and not governed like the Colonies by these pampered pompous Protestant pusillanimous pukes that keep pestering our way of life. For the sake of their Christ I was retired, sort of. I did try!" Edward said with raucous laughter.

"Jackson, take Juliet and your daughter Josephine and make haste to the Territory of Orleans. Once there, meet us at the Mississippi. Take this purse, it's overflowing with gold and silver. There is more than enough to get you to the Mississippi river. Heck, my boy if you spend sparingly you should have enough to get settled. We shall make haste ourselves, God willing there's a breeze at our back."

Jack, sensing great danger reluctantly said his farewells and as quickly as a greyhound sprinted back to the aft of the ship. Instead of climbing back down the ladder, he leaped off the railing, executed a full-on dive submerging underneath the water, before ultimately breaking the surface. He then swam the short distance back to Ocracoke.

Chapter One. New Orleans, Louisiana, 2002, Decatur Street.

A man, roughly six feet tall, with broad shoulders and a thin physique walked casually up and down Decatur Street on the city's Mississippi side periodically stopping and staring at a particular two-story building. He admired its beautiful French, Spanish and Creole architecture. He also admired its beautiful wrought iron balcony and magnificent cypress storm shutters. White washed and faded with age, they complimented the black and white tile that arched out from the front door.

A Mercantile Shop: "Madame Juliette's", was plainly spelled out on a beautifully hand-forged gothic wrought iron sign.

The man had long, sandy blonde hair and a thick, untrimmed beard. He wore a light-weight black leather jacket, leather riding gloves, blue jeans and black well-worn leather cowboy boots. His hat was a dusty, old black Stetson. Pulled low over his wide-set piercing blue eyes, it looked like it could have come straight out of a western movie. Clasped around his neck and tucked under his shirt was a pure silver rope chain with multiple charms and amulets clamped onto it. At first glance, he gave the impression of being a perpetual traveler, not exactly a vagabond, but not homeless either.

He vividly recalled the time when the building in front of him was constructed in 1720. The French had just established the settlement, "La Nouvelle-Orleans" and with the purse Blackbeard had given him on The Adventure he was flush with wealth.

He hired members of the local Chitimacha, a band of First People on the continent to help with construction. The Chitmacha had inhabited the land six-thousand-plus years before Europeans arrived. He appreciated them and they appreciated him. He paid them well and in return they showed him their special technique for treating the cyprus he had sourced from local forests. Something he'd come to appreciate throughout the centuries.

He also remembered, first hand, when the Spanish assumed control of the settlement from the French in 1762 and ruled for 40 years afterwards, leaving the British out of the equation. He remembered too, the fire that devastated New Orleans in 1788 and the smaller one that followed in the mid-1790s.

Afterwards, his family was forced to add stucco and fire-retardant roofing to comply with Spanish ordinances. The result was a perfect blend of old-world French, Colonial Spanish and Caribbean influences.

He helped his family commission the wrought iron balcony and was thrilled at how beautiful it looked with all of its intricate metal work that flowed into the black and white tile archway. A blend of obsidian and Greek marble, he had painstakingly cut and placed each of them, one at a time. In homage to the original French settlement, he designed an accompanying fleur-de-lis emblem and integrated it with his family's coat of arms. He also had some subtle symbols of prosperity, health and protection forged into the iron.

The charms, spells and woodworking techniques the Chitmacha shared worked their magic. The shop had survived both fires, several hurricanes, rot, war, rioting, looting, Mardi Gras parades and overall French Quarter debauchery through the centuries.

"Vieux Carré!" he said with a sigh of nostalgia. He stood for a while and stared at the shop's front door while contemplating whether it would be wise to go in and try to engage the owner about their shared history now, or later. He came by several weeks earlier to place an order for ingredients and supplies he needed to make a salve.

She had been tending to another customer at that moment, so he simply jotted his order down on a notepad he found on the counter and left it there along with a small stack of $20 bills before departing. He was confident that she would understand the money was to pay for his order.

<u>*Chapter Two. NOLA 2002, Late October.*</u>

"Hello, welcome back!" a young woman standing behind the counter, dressed in black yoga pants and a gray Tulane University sweatshirt responded to the front door opening and a little silver bell ringing.

Upon entering, the man recalled when he'd put the little bell in place as a high-level charm of protection.

The store sported highly polished cedar flooring and red brick walls that were covered partially with drywall. Hand carved and polished crown molding lined the walls. A large aluminum ceiling fan with wooden blades hung low at midpoint. In the northwest corner of the shop stood a beautifully hand-forged, wrought iron spiral staircase. Shelves lining most of the two walls adjacent to the counter were festooned with various eclectic and occultist items, including chicken feet keychains, Voodoo dolls, shrunken heads, pixie dust, charms, amulets and potions, along with some hardback books, magazines, CDs, DVDs and VHS tapes. A portable clothing rack held scarves, shirts and jackets. Next to the clothing rack stood an enclosed glass jewelry case. The goods were procured from local haberdashers, tailors, artists and jewelry makers. None came from Big Box suppliers. Julie's clientele appreciated the fact that she maintained a wide arrayof connections from which to source and find whatever they wanted. Most of the time, anyway.

"Ahh, you remember me?" the man said reservedly.

"Of course," she replied. "We couldn't get everything on your list, but we were able to get most of what you needed. I'm glad you're back, we never caught your name."

She often referred to herself in the plural to give shoppers and lookiloos the impression that there were other employees onboard. It was a matter of safety.

"I'm very pleased!" he said. "Do, pray tell though, what's missing from the lot?"

"We were unable to get the exact species of silkworm you requested, but I did find it's very close cousin. They're about a 98 percent genetic match. Are you trying to produce a salve?, she asked in a straightforward manner, "does it have to be an exact recipe?"

"No," he replied and looked away for a few seconds as he contemplated whether or not he had enough of what he needed. "This should work, but I may have to dilute a couple things. Anyway, how did you figure it out?"

"I guess I'm just pretty good at putting two and two together," she said with a devil-may-care look on her face.

You're definitely an empath and a mind reader, he thought, without saying so.

"Look Mr.?" she interjected as she raised her left eyebrow in a quizzical manner.

"Jack," he replied, matter of factly.

"Do you care to tell me your last name, Jack?"

He hesitated as he weighed the timing. It's too early. She'll think I'm a lunatic and kick me out of the store. But he was ready to take that risk until he noticed that her expression had suddenly changed from congeniality to impatience.

"Mr. Jack, here in New Orleans some people only have one name and it seems Jack is yours!" she said flatly. "Well, Mr. Jack, is there any other business we can conduct today? Mr. Jack? Mr. Jack, are you all right, sir?"

He appeared uneasy on his feet as he grabbed the edge of the counter.

"Um, yes. Yes, I'm alright, I just can't believe how much you look like her!"

"Like her? Sir, you are an odd duck! Even for New AHL-lee-ins," she said in a heavy accent.

"I apologize," Jack replied. "My full name is Jackson Tiberius Worthington the 3rd, born in Kingston, Jamaica, 1692. I'm your great, great, great, great, grandfather."

Chapter Three. NOLA 2002, The Mercantile Shop.

A brief, yet uncomfortable silence ensued between the shopkeeper and her customer before she insisted that he leave.

"Sir! Jack! Or whoever the hell you are, I don't think your joke is the least bit funny and I'd appreciate it if you just grabbed your things and left. There are plenty of other stores in New Orleans you can patronize. Please do not come back here again. Now, leave before I call the police!"

"Juliette Anne Marie Louviere," Jack said, "You have her eyes. Your complexion is lighter, though. Please, I can prove it to you, just give me a moment to explain. I shouldn't have jumped right into it. God damn it. I should have waited!"

"I don't recall giving you my name sir!" Julie said, her eyes beaming like lasers. "You have five minutes to tell your story. Then I'll decide whether or not to call the police. You appear to know a bit about my family. But you could have dug that up on the internet..."

Jack cut her short. "What's on the internet or in public records about our family is very limited and mostly BS. It's only what we wanted the world to know about us. The truth is far more complex. I can tell it to you if you just relax."

"Don't tell me to relax. You came in here out of nowhere, claiming to be my 310-year-old grandfather from five generations ago. New Orleans is a crazy place, full of crazy people, but you sir are the powdered sugar on the beignet."

Jack contemplated his response for a couple minutes, then looked her straight in the eyes and dove right in. ~

"Your ancestor, Juliette, and I were born in the same house at the same time, June 7, 1692, 11:43 a.m. Legend has it that there was a powerful earthquake at the moment of our births. I researched it later and confirmed that it was true. My father was Baron Jackson Tiberius Worthington the 2nd. My mother was Baroness Evelyn Rose Dubois.

"In a separate room, a baby girl was born to a different

mother. She was your great-great-great-great-

grandmother, Juliette Anne Marie LaRue.

Juliette's mother was a slave, purchased along with a

dozen others, from Saint Domingue, known today as

Haiti. She was brought to the island of Jamaica and

taught to cook.

"My father was once thought to be your father as well.

But, as it turned out, the overseer, Ricardo Guzman

Bustamante Martinez, was her father.

"Ricardo was from El Puerto De Santa Maria, España. His family relocated to Spanish Town, Jamaica, when he was 5 years old. Ricardo was educated up until 12 years of age when his family deemed him old enough to find employment. He then signed on with the Worthington's plantation as a stable boy and worked his way up to the position of overseer.

"During a card game my father was overheard to say braggadociously that he honestly couldn't remember if he'd slept with the cook or not. The cook, on the other hand, swore it never happened.

"The overseer had slept with the cook, but in the interest of not damaging his reputation, she kept it a secret, since it was essential that he maintain a high standard of respect on the Worthington's plantation.

"The truth is that the overseer was actually quite a gentle soul. He would only dole out punishment to those truly deserving. Thieves, rapists and on one occasion, a murderer. Yet, his chief concern was enforcing a fair code of rules and ethics and, in so doing, he was one of the key players in the success of the plantation.

"Juliette and I were as thick as thieves while growing up. We were inseparable. Our respective caregivers even bathed us together as tots. We slept in the same room up until we were 10 years of age. After our 11th year, we were given rooms right next to one another.

"Juliette began her training as a house stewardess and I started my studies in classical education. I was told I had what was called an eidetic memory and quickly excelled through the grades. It's impossible for me to forget anything. I taught her to read and write. She taught me how to cook.

"Juliette was incredibly gifted when it came to understanding people and their emotions. I was aware that the women in her bloodline were powerful, some more so than others. Their lineage practiced Voodoo. Most maintained, albeit incognito, their West African spiritual traditions.~

"Voodoo, or in the case of Juliette's ancestry, was really Vodún, a religion that teaches its followers to worship many different entities around a single recognized god. And in so doing they will speak to God on their behalf.

"Vodún centers around the spirits and other elements of the divine essence that govern Earth. It is a hierarchy that includes major deities atop the forces of nature and human society, down to the spirits of nature, including individual streams, trees, and rocks. There are also dozens of ethnic Vodún, defenders of certain clans,-tribes, and nations. The Vodún are the center of religious life. The guiding principle of Vodún is that what you pray for to the inaccessible god, refocuses towards the Vodún, or spirits. They are his representatives and will give a report to him on your behalf. Vodún aims at capturing all visible and invisible forces, in order to bring everything into harmony.

"Juliette and I were unaware of it at the time, but we were meant to be together from the very beginning, an invisible force unto ourselves, manifested by love.~

"One Sunday afternoon when we were in our teens, I'd gone looking for her after church and found her down by the river washing out some garments. I snuck up behind and grabbed her. She was startled and we then fell to the ground laughing as we rolled around on the riverbed.

"Unexpectedly, Juliette, not quite sure of what she was doing, pushed me onto my back, wrapped her legs around my belly and planted a kiss on my lips. I was surprised, but also aroused and didn't fight or hesitate to kiss her back. The kiss couldn't have lasted more than 30-45 seconds, but it felt much longer to me. Right then and there I fell in love with her. Fact is, I always had been and always would be. I also knew that she was in love with me and that she'd be mine for eternity."

At this point, Jack stopped his narrative, looked at the pocket watch he pulled from his jacket and said with a mock reproachful glance, "It appears my 5 minutes are up and since I wish to not have a hole blown through my chest I believe I'll bid you adieu. Au revoir Ma-"

Julie immediately interrupted him. "I've done a lot of research and collected everything I could from Jamaica to New Orleans and abroad to figure out who my family are," she said. "There have been many roadblocks and a great deal of missing information. I assume you might attest to deliberately blurring this history for your own selfish sake.

"Make no mistake, I still think your story is hogwash, but I also believe you know some important details about my family's lineage, and I'm willing to listen. What can I lose? You may stay. I'll lock the doors and make us tea. Sit down, we have some talking to do."

She waltzed off, locked the front door and then proceeded to the galley, her ponytail swaying back and forth.

"I prepared green, white and black tea. I don't know which one you'd like, so I brought all three," Julie said while placing a service tray on the cocktail table in the lounge where Jack was sitting.

"Black is fine. I take it with just a little milk please," Jack responded, trying his best to sound casual. He was reminiscing over a painting he commissioned in 1821 that still hung in the parlor of the shop. An oil on canvas, it was a beautiful landscape of Lake Pontchartrain and it's various bird species, vibrantly detailed. He remembered meeting the young and penniless Autobahn. The poor young artist whom he commissioned had just had his pockets picked in the Quarter. After spending time with him, Jack was not surprised by the acclaim that he received throughout the scientific community and the United States during the last couple of centuries. He also recalled arguments they had pertaining to the abolitionist movement, John James Audubon being opposed. Jack remembers visiting him in 1850 in New York City and thinking how out of place Audubon seemed and that he clearly held to Southern values of the time.

After their tea steeped for a few minutes, Jack continued his story.

Jamaica.

"As I stated, we were in love and always wanted to be together. Our parents, both mine and hers, seemed to allow us our freedom. I was alone with my mother one evening. Father happened to be away on business and she asked me how I felt about marriage. I replied to her that I planned to marry Juliette and was waiting for the right opportunity to ask them for their blessing. To my surprise and utter dismay, my mother became quite angry. She told me that my plan was ungodly and unheard of and father would never allow it! I should forget the very idea."

Jack paused for a moment, looked Julie straight in the eyes and said, "She forbade me to marry the love of my life. She said it would be an abomination to God and his will! My mother told me that if I had any intentions of marrying the half-breed, father would disown me."

NOLA.

Tears welled up in Jack's eyes and he looked away from Julie in shame. As sympathy overcame her feelings of distrust, Julie walked over to Jack and put her arm around him. It was just then that she noticed he smelled like decaying flesh and figured he must be very near death.

Jack was only too aware of his body odor, yet he continued his narrative.

Jamaica.

"I was appalled and frustrated that my own mother would stoop so low. I told her she was a horrible mother and I didn't love her. Both were untrue. I ran straight to my room and knocked on Juliette's door next to mine. When she answered I didn't say a thing, I just grabbed her by the arm and pulled her downstairs. Mother stood downstream by the banister with a glass of rum in her right hand and a bemused look on her face. 'Be back before father gets home,' was all she said. We raced to one of our favorite hiding spots in the woods. Right then and there I went down on my knees and asked her if she would marry me.

'No, we are too young and besides I heard the fight you had with your mother,' she said. 'She doesn't think I'm worthy of your family. I'm a half-breed, a slave girl. She's probably right.'

"We both cried. I felt completely defeated, so I turned away from her and ran as fast as I could and didn't stop until I reached the harbor. I was so exhausted by the time I hit the shore I passed out. I'm not sure exactly how many hours I slept but it wasn't until the next morning that father and his hunting party found me shivering cold and half dead. They wrapped blankets around me and placed me over the back of his horse where I passed out again. Upon returning home, father excused his men and escorted their horses and his into the stable. I was fully awake by then. As punishment, I was ordered to care for the horses. I was rested. I could handle the task. I replenished their hay and- filled their pails with fresh water. I also checked their hooves and brushed out their hides, manes and tails.

"There were five horses in total. About an hour later, father came out and informed me that mother had told him everything. He lectured me about carnal love and duty to one's family and how duty sometimes supersedes love even though love feels like the path one should follow. He concluded his sermon by further detailing what was expected of me.

"He made it painfully clear that I was to have nothing to do with Juliette aside from friendship and even in that role I would continue to be her master and benefactor. He asked me if I still wanted to be a surgeon and when I replied in the affirmative, he then stated that his connections to the Royal College of Physicians of London, my scholastic abilities and his money would more than guarantee my education.

"I felt a mix of emotions. I was tired and confused by the entire situation. I was unable to marry the love of my life because my parents would never accept her into their world. I was 15 years old and heartbroken. It was the year 1707 and summer was running out. But I very much looked forward to the possibility of a challenging and rewarding career.

"I asked my father when I could depart to England whereupon he laughed and told me, 'As soon as God wills it, we will see you on your way!"

<u>*Chapter Four. London. 1707-1713.*</u>

<u>*NOLA*</u>

"London was a virtual world away from the lifestyle of Jamaica in the early 1700s," Jack said while pausing to take in the decor of Madame Juliette's parlor.

"This building was originally constructed of old-growth cypress. Those trees are long gone," he said with a tone of melancholy.

Jack was content to keep talking until he noticed Julie sniffling. The odor of his bodily decay was obviously bothering her.

"I'm sorry. My body odor is one of the reasons I'm here. I need to use the salve, as I ordered. I also take multiple showers daily if I am able. In the industrialized era, I have to say indoor plumbing was a godsend for my condition."

With grace and tact, Julie moved back to her original seat and Jack continued his narrative.

Jamaica to England. 1707.

"I had four weeks to get ready for my voyage. Preparations were needed not only as far as supplies for the voyage, but also for what I would need for several years while attending university. Besides the obvious trunks full of clothing for the various seasons, books and my riding saddle, I packed any and all essentials I thought I couldn't live without. I packed and then often repacked until I was satisfied.

"In addition to material supplies, I was gifted a virtual treasure trove of coins and gems. Silver, gold trinkets, goblets and whatnot. I was told the money would be enough to last 20 years in London if I lived modestly and it would certainly be enough to survive five to seven while attending school.

"I felt like a pirate! All of this booty was in a trunk with chains wrapped around it, locked. I was about to embark on a sea voyage through the Caribbean and across the Atlantic. I was sure to see pirates along the way, or I hoped anyway. We'd had privateers in our family, cousins from the island or at least one cousin in particular.

"I was also informed that I would be traveling with two bodyguards. Men handpicked by my father who were part of his hunting brigade. They were to accompany me to London and see that I settled comfortably before returning home. The journey itself was unremarkable as far as sea voyages were concerned. We saw absolutely nothing, not a pirate ship, not even a vessel from another kingdom. What I did see were several- different types of whales, a few pods of dolphins chasing our vessel and the biggest turtle God ever put breath in.

"We made it to London in 21 days. It was remarkable in the fact that not a single raindrop hit us the entire way and we seemed to always have plenty of wind in our sails. The older, salty dogs commented on what good fortune we were having while a few stated it must be an omen. Of what, they weren't sure, but all agreed they'd never seen better weather and sailing conditions.

Once landed, preparations were made to rent me an apartment flat and for my booty to be guarded by the Bank of London, whereupon I was allocated an allowance. I was enrolled in school via the letter my father wrote the schoolmaster and I immediately got into my new routine.

Most days were uneventful. School work, fencing, rowing and reading required literature, as well as that which wasn't required. For fun and exercise, I trained in bare-knuckle boxing and even had several bouts at the Royal Theater of London. I won a few purses and spent my winnings frequenting the local pubs.

I made friends and acquaintances along the way. I particularly enjoyed the company of older folks who occupied their time at the tea houses while playing chess, a game I learned easily and excelled at.

I got into some skirmishes with older boys who may have been jealous that I was so accomplished scholastically at such a young age. Several bouts of fisticuffs in back alleys of London gave me the utmost appreciation for my bare-knuckle boxing training.

Nonetheless, my marks in school were excellent and my studies progressed at breakneck speed. Ultimately, I accepted an offer to contribute to the curriculum itself. My hypotheses and theories revolved around the need for sanitation and sterilization of medical instruments and facilities. We knew that keeping a wound clean would help the healing process. Why not start off with sterilizing hospitals, clinics and equipment?

"Fall and winter were cold, foggy and wet in London. Spring and summer were a reprieve, but still much, much cooler than where I came from.

"Regardless of the weather, time seemed to fly by at the speed of light. Three years quickly turned into four, four into five and inevitably six. I graduated with honors and was asked to stay on as an instructor. As tempting as that was, my life was back in Jamaica and I was ready to go home. I missed my family, my friends and most of all Juliette. I was 21 years of age, a full-grown man. I was ready to get back and take over the family business. Arrangements were made and I was homeward bound."

London to Jamaica.

"Like the trip going there, the trip coming home was uneventful. We didn't see a single pirate ship, nor any other vessels, for that matter. Of course the weather cooperated. We had ample wind at our sails, but still did not have to endure rain.

"The trip took 29 days this time, still unremarkable. I later found out that Juliette had given me a charm made for travelers and hid it deep within my sea chest. She explained how it warded off danger and ensured safety for the ship's occupants.

"I was welcomed back with open arms. My father's sailors were more than happy to have me aboard. I was considered a good luck charm, or a good omen, if you will.

"On our first day out of port, the boatswain's mate stated that he knew it was going to be easy sailing because I was here and for reasons known to the Almighty, I was protected.

"To my amazement, I saw that huge turtle again. It was almost like it came up to say hello and I swear it winked at me before it dove back below the surface.

"We docked the morning of the 29th day and to my delight, my parents and a few members of my father's hunting brigade were there to greet me. I ran down the gangplank and embraced my mother and father with hugs and kisses and may have embarrassed my father with too much emotion. I even hugged some of his men, who seemed unsure of what to do, but hugged me in return.

"We took our time getting back to the plantation, talking about everything under the sun except the Sun. Mother and father brought me up to speed with goings on regarding the plantation and our shipping business. Apparently, we were doing exceptionally well. We did-lose one ship to privateers. The loss of the crew was the most detrimental aspect, spiritually and financially. Word had it our merchant sailors were unceremoniously dumped into the sea to swim for their lives. A witness claimed the pirates made-sport of it, taking bets on who would be able to keep their head above water the longest. The captain took unfair advantage by shooting the merchant sailors to hedge his bets.

"Mind boggling! Man's inhumanity to man.

"After arriving at the main house on horseback, my belongings were stored, and the horses were taken to the stables. Mother escorted me into the parlor and father excused himself to tend to matters of the estate.

"You look incredibly well rested for a man who just spent the better part of a month at sea,'" my mother said with a wry smile.

"Like I said, it was uneventful, a bit of a bore, really. But, I learned a lot about sailing and the open sea, different rigs, ropes, knots and various apparatuses. I may even ask the harbor master for more opportunities. Truth be told mother, I'm exhausted and I need to rest," I said while faking a yawn. I really just wanted to be by myself.

"I needed to gather some strength before I spoke with Juliette. I kissed my mom on the forehead and proceeded upstairs to my room. To my delight nothing had changed. Everything was exactly how I left it. I laid down upon my bed and found sleep more quickly than I anticipated.

"I woke up later that evening to a rapping on my door and a soft voice saying, 'Masta Worthington, Masta Worthington, dinner suh. Suh, is you up? Do you need assistance?'"

"'No thank you JoJo. Tell everyone I'll be down in a minute and to go ahead and start without me, I just need to freshen up,'" I told him. JoJo left without a reply.

"He'd been in the service of my family his whole life. At 5 feet, 2 inches in height and as black as the night, he was often underestimated. Yet, the man was as sharp as a tack! He was allowed to self-educate and he attended basic schooling up until he was 15 years of age. Interesting fella. We conversed often. He was especially knowledgeable about history, although he-was sure that the history books got more than a few things wrong.

"I was utterly flabbergasted upon entering our formal dining room. It appeared the whole island was here. Everybody turned around and started clapping and congratulating me. Salutations came from left and right, not only in English but Spanish and French as well.

"There was a fantastic cornucopia of different food items. Roasted pig on a spit, chicken, quail and other fowl prepared in different culinary techniques. Seafood dishes I recognized as shark, eel, crab, and crustaceans of various sizes. The plethora of different side dishes, crudites and accompaniments were so abundant I started to question if there was any food left on the island. Father had his best wine brought up from the cellars and at least 12 barrels of mead.

"The sights and smells were magnificent. Here I was, back from London, educated, a full-grown man and yet, I was about to cry because my family, my friends and the entire island welcomed me home in such grandiose fashion! I was overwhelmed.

"After 15 minutes or so, the crowd settled down and I was escorted to my seat. I was placed at the right-hand side of my father at the head of the table. I was only too aware that meant I was deemed heir apparent, an obvious promotion.

"Our table was full of dignitaries, heads of state, an earl, barrons and various wealthy tycoons and aristocrats. I was pleased to see a distant cousin in the mix. It was rumored, but never confirmed, that he was a privateer.

Nevermind the scuttlebutt, I simply wanted to talk to him about life on the open sea. Juliette was nowhere to be found. I questioned my father as to her whereabouts, yet he brushed me off. After a couple hours of eating and drinking I found an opportunity to excuse myself from the table and meander through the crowd.

"I encountered friends and family members and engaged in frivolous conversation. I tried to keep it light. I spotted my cousin in the middle of the crowd and made a beeline toward him.
'Edward Teach!' I said excitedly while shaking his hand a bit too enthusiastically.

"Edward, I must say it's absolutely fantastic to see you, cousin! I haven't seen you since I was 10 years old."

"Jack Worthington, or more appropriately, Master Jack Tiberius Worthington the 3rd. You sir are looking more like a full-grown gentleman than ever before. You've really filled out, young man!"

"Does your mother allow tobacco in the house?" Edward asked very nonchalantly.

"I'm afraid not, it gives her headaches," I said apologetically. "Let's go to the terrace, the fresh air will do us good and you can smoke to your heart's content."

"Fantastic idea, lad! You're a mighty fine host and will make an excellent head of the table when your father retires." He said this with a wry grin on his face.

"Notice my placement tonight, eh?"

"You'd have to be a blind, deaf, dumb imbecile not to have. I did notice a few of that variety at this evening's gathering though, hahaha...!"

"Edward nearly doubled over with self-induced laughter. I couldn't help but chuckle. The man was vibrant and enthusiastic.

"He was verbose but tactful. He was charming, educated and worldly. Despite being 12 years my senior I believe he had 10 times my energy. He was able to give the impression of being tough, mean and calculated on the exterior.

"But under that demeanor was one of the most loyal and caring persons you'd ever want to meet. He sported a long dreadlock beard, obsidian black. He wore a black, cavalier hat, conspicuously cocked to the right that held a beautiful long ostrich feather. The crown was encircled with jewels.

"Typical for men of his stature, he was dressed in a black, cutaway tailored coat with silver buttons over a waist-length satin waistcoat, white shirt and black breeches. Black leather boots with silver buckles completed the outfit.

"He was passionate about shooting guns, fighting, and swordplay. He had served on merchant ships and sailed with the Royal Navy starting in his mid-20s.

"'Rumor has it you're a privateer going by the name of Blackbeard! I heard you were 8 feet tall, solid rock muscle and as mean as a 300-year-old crocodile. I also heard you eat the hearts of your enemy to gain their strength." I couldn't keep from laughing.

"'I remember when I was really young I used to call you Blackbeard because of your facial hair. But am I to understand that's your pirate name?" I asked sincerely but feared it may have come out mockingly.

"Edward just looked at me and said, 'Reputation is everything and mine seems to proceed me!' His thunderous laughter echoed off the walls and ceiling of the terrace.

<u>*NOLA. 2002*</u>.

"Wait, wait a second, hold on!" Julie interrupted in the parlor of the shop where she was having tea with Jack. The Blackbeard! The notorious scoundrel pirate Blackbeard? The murderous thug and scourge of the Caribbean, Blackbeard?

"Yes, the one and only, but understand, history had him all wrong. Mostly because Edward had designed a fake persona in order to create fear and hopelessness throughout the Colonies and the Caribbean. It was easier for people to be afraid and just hand things over instead of him having to murder them. He also had a Robin Hood complex. Most likely would have been a philanthropist today who made his money on Wall Street," Jack said with a snicker.

<u>**Chapter Six. NOLA 2002.**</u>

"Are you hungry, Julie asked?"

"Quite, what did you have in mind?"

Julie contemplated for a moment and then said, "How about Commander's Palace, my treat? I'd like to get out of the Quarta', as you know, late October in New Orleans can hold on to the heat like an overprotective mother, lucky for us it's starting to cool off. It's going to be a pleasant evening and Commander's Palace has a beautiful outdoor patio. We'll have to get you some-clothing, It's a little higher end. Francois the maître d' is a close friend of mine. I'll call and make a reservation.

"The restaurant makes their weekend gumbo on Thursday and today is Friday. It's a Cajun gumbo not Creole. The Cajuns say that it's best when the ingredients have married and gone through their honeymoon before you eat the gumbo ya! Ça c'est bon, Monsieur!" Julie said as she kissed the tip of her fingers in an outward gesture.

Jack smiled, bowed and replied, "I have a trunk hidden in Jackson Square that has a fine suit that would be perfect for an evening out in the Quarta' on a Friday, Cher!"

They laughed simultaneously and decided that Julie should come help him retrieve his trunk. They exited the store and hooked a right, walked about a block and turned right again on St. Ann, crossed the street and walked into Jackson Square Park. The park smelled faintly of urine and alcohol. The "parfum de choix" of New Orleans. Most of the street artists had gone home or elsewhere. There were a few young black performers tap dancing on the sidewalk. A musician was blowing his horn. Stragglers and drunks meandered as dusk crept in.

"It's kind of dark, Jack. I don't see a trunk anywhere. Wait hold on what's that, over there behind the oak tree? That's it isn't it? Where the hell did that thing come from? I swear to God I looked there just a moment ago and there was nothing! Jack?"

Julie was both excited and exasperated. She cupped her mouth with her left hand.

"It's enchanted by a mid-level spell that only a few are allowed to see," Jack explained. "I've had this particular trunk for just over 100 years and amazingly, I've been able to tote it around with zero problems. It's my life, I'll show you. Here, grab the side and let's get this upstairs, you said there's still a bedroom upstairs, correct?" Jack asked.

"You bet. I actually just had the curtains cleaned and the carpet shampooed. You've got great timing!" Julie replied pridefully.

Jack had purchased the large impressive E. Goyard

steamer trunk in Paris, France, in 1900. It was dome

shaped and covered in signature Goyard chevron

canvas. The locks and hardware had patinated to a

beautiful rosy rust and moss green color. When the

steamer trunk was opened Jack pointed out the original

fitted interior with Goyard leather pulls. He showed her

the six ascending drawers and how each time he took

one out it was automatically and mystically replaced by

another. He also showed her the original wood hangers,

canvas shoe pouches and leather accessory holders.

All still had their original leather straps. It stood on four

casters and had all the original Goyard hardware and

fittings. Again, he showed her the anomaly of the

drawers, extracting an item out from inside the trunk

while another item of equal value and importance

magically appeared in its place. He returned the item, -

thus exemplifying how the one in place before had suddenly disappeared.

"The trunk has a mind of its own. Sometimes it refuses to give me the items I requested," he said. "I originally charmed it to anticipate my needs but we've never been able to psychically connect 100 percent of the time. I do have to say though, it has about a 75 percent accuracy rate. In your house, it's buzzing with energy. I feel a very strong connection to it. It's the reason we built on this exact location. It's a bottomless well of harmonious energy, incredibly well balanced."

Inundated and engulfed by the entire ordeal Julie said, "I feel like I'm in a dream! Jack, am I dreaming?"

Julie had beautiful emerald green eyes, almost an exact match to his Juliette. Her features were perfectly symmetrical. With a button nose, soft high cheeks and a well-defined, proud chin. Julie was very comley. She had cocoa brown skin and shiny black hair she wore in a ponytail that bobbed up and down when she walked.

"I'm afraid you're as wide awake as a barn owl at midnight looking for lunch," Jack said in a manner he hoped came across as concerned, grandfatherly love. Yet he feared sounded more like a backwoods redneck colloquialism.

Julie let out the most pleasant laugh and between cute little snorts said, "I'll be back in an hour, do your thing. The shower gets plenty hot. There are fresh clean towels in the closet. I use this place as a quasi-guest house when company comes to town or I have a date that I don't know well just yet and do not wish to bring-back to my real home. I have a mansion on St. Anne.

It's been in my family, or if you're for real, I mean our

family for a few generations."

Jack knew the place, of course, but responded tactfully,

"I'm familiar with the mansion on St Ann. An hour

should be perfect! I'll arrange a carriage for us."

"Umm, a carriage, really? Well we are going to

Commander's Palace. Sounds good, I'll see you in an

hour! You know how to use a phone and whatnot?" she

replied with a teasing granddaughter-like smile.

"I'm old, but not dead!" he replied.

**Chapter Six. NOLA 2002**.

Jack rummaged through several different suits until he settled on a slim-cut charcoal Armani. The trunk brought it into rotation and admittedly the trunk was correct. He chose a classic starched white button down shirt with modern French cuffs and collar. Pure silver fleur-de-lis cufflinks. Salvatore Ferragamo classic black leather oxfords. A charcoal Armani silk tie with black paisley embroidery. Thomas Ested, London Oignon silver pocket watch, Champleve dial. Circa 1700. A gift from his late father. Finished with an Eton white silk pocket square embroidered with a small but visible black fleur-de-lis.

"When in Rome," he thought. He also grabbed enough cash for three nights out. He wanted Julie to have a wonderful time. He had showered, scrubbed, salved, deodorized and perfumed his body. He trimmed his beard neatly and reflected on how his blonde hair and beard had mostly stayed the same color throughout the centuries. His hair was slicked back and pulled into a man bun. To his dismay, he detected a slightly green tinge to his hair when he got up close to the mirror, yet with a little spray-on product it was hardly noticeable. His eyes were still piercing blue and while his vision was sharp, they reflected his exhaustion. His nose was angular, not big, but not small and his cheekbones were well defined. He mastered long ago a blend of different applications- and tones of makeup that allowed him the appearance of a youthful complexion. His looks were now betrayed merely by his old-school mannerisms, vernacular and character. He double checked the time-on his freshly wound and set pocket watch, heard mules neighing and clamping their hoofs on the cobblestone drive and was pleased to have reserved the carriage. He retrieved his Egyptian white cotton dinner gloves and made his way down to the parlor.

Jack was pouring himself a 21-year-old single malt Glen Fiddich in a crystal rocks glass when Julie walked in to the ring of the little silver bell and proclaimed, "Your carriage has arrived sir! Impressive, I didn't think we were going to get one on a Friday night."

Jack smiled and said, "I told them it was your 21st birthday and what a bad brother I was to forget. I also told the dispatcher I'd pay extra if they would be so kind as to send one our way promptly."

"Shall we be off then?" Julie asked, extending her elbow

towards Jack.

"Indeed." Jack said, as he finished off his drink,

received her arm in his and escorted her out the door.

Julie let go of his arm briefly to lock up the shop and

said, "You certainly clean up well, Mr. Jack!" She

hesitated a moment before adding, "You claim to be

over 300 years old yet looking at you I'd swear you're in

your mid-20s. By the way, you smell fabulous, much

better than earlier. I'm enjoying hearing about our

family. I trust somehow we are connected, but you're

going to have to tell me more. I'd like to find out how

and why you're still alive. What's all this magic talk and

how did you get that trunk upstairs to perform tricks? I

know I've got a million other questions, but I think those

are the most important for now. I reserved a nice quiet

table. My friend Francois is on duty and will see to our-dinner this evening. I'm delighted you're here and I hope that you'll be honest and truthful with me."

Jack stopped, turned to face Julie, rested both of his hands reassuringly on her shoulders and looked her over for the second time.

She was wearing a classic Valentino black and red cocktail dress. Black silk upper bodice and sleeves. Deep V-neck. Red satin cumberbund and black velvet skirt. Sakura Marsala - T-strap sandals, red Bordeaux leather. She was adorned with a 24-karat gold antique chain from which hung a genuine 5 karat blood red ruby pendant. She carried a Louis Vuitton black and red clutch bag at her side.

Jack's heart skipped a beat at the sight of the pendant. He knew it well.

"Of course, I'll be honest with you, it won't work any other way. I've been honest with you 100 percent so far. I'll explain more over dinner," Jack said with candor.

After helping Julie into the carriage, Jack walked around the back and climbed aboard.

"The driver just let me know that our destination is farther than is customary for him, so I slipped him some extra cash and said I'll take care of anything and everything."

"High roller!" Julie quipped. "For a man who appeared to be a vagabond a few hours ago you're looking and acting mighty affluent," she said with a laugh.

"You my dear are looking ever so much the A-lister this evening as well. Belle of the ball!" Jack said with his best American nouveau riche accent.

Slightly embarrassed Julie felt compelled to explain.

"Francoise's boyfriend owns a vintage clothing store on Bourbon. These are great finds, he probably sold them-to me for less than he paid for them. I always make it up and have them over for dinner whenever possible. You'll have to meet Christopher, He's fabulous! Jack smiled and decided to give Julie some more information.

"I had to fake my death in 1750 and since then I've worn many different hats while living in the shadows. Downtrodden is a great way to hide in plain sight. I accumulated and maintained wealth for the family through good investments, hard work and a bit of luck. I steered away from greed as best I could. When the coffers became too large and noticeable I would have our lawyers donate large sums of money to charitable organizations and or entities of my choosing. Sometimes I would follow the recommendations of the lawyers. Our lawyers are all related to us in some form or fashion. To work at our firm, you have to be blood.-

They know our secrets and are sworn to protect them. They're also compensated incredibly well for their silence and loyalty. So far, to date, not one leak has ever materialized. I stashed some money away on the side for my own well-being but it pales in comparison to what is in our trust." Jack said proudly.

"Trust? Lawyers? I don't follow," Julie questioned.

"The shop and your house are valued roughly at $500,000 but you already knew that and they're yours and yours alone. I've set aside about $1 million in cash in a couple of- different offshore accounts. Our land in Jamaica is worth close to $3 million and our interest in the family shipping business is close to $1 million and a half. We also own a small law firm headquartered in New Iberia, named "Jackson and Associates." Valued at roughly $750,000," Jack said smiling.

The carriage was moving from roughly a south by southwest direction on Decatur Street. The Mississippi was to the left and Jean Lafitte National Historical Park was on their right as they passed by.

"I knew Jean." Jack said, breaking the silence.

"Pardon?" Julie replied.

"Jean Lafitte, the pirate and his older brother Pierre," he said.

"Of course, you must have known a lot of pirates," she said jokingly.

"A few, but Jean Lafitte was one of my favorites, second only to Blackbeard. Lafitte sailed for Andrew Jackson and helped defend New Orleans during the War of 1812. He also became a spy in the Mexican War of Independence. Notorious and infamous he and his fellow privateers gained the admiration and respect of Jackson. I met them here in New Orleans. They were smugglers. I helped Lafitte bury his treasure on Jefferson- Island, close to New Iberia. Story has it that a slave girl unearthed it and was never seen afterwards." He said the last part with a mischievous look on his face.

The journey took them over Canal Street where they merged onto Magazine, passed under Highway 90 then took a right on Erato, left on Prytania and ultimately hit Washington Street in the Garden District of Uptown New Orleans where they stopped at Commander's Palace. A Victorian mansion, or more colloquially,-

"Victorian Cuckoo", it was painted a vibrant, deep teal, complemented by an equally cheery white-striped awning.

On the other side of Washington lies Lafayette Cemetery. One of the oldest city-governed cemeteries. The cemetery was named after the city of Lafayette, Louisiana, which was once inside the Area of New Orleans.
With almost 500 wall vaults the cemetery has a rich history.
Jack couldn't help but reminisce. Several friends and one relative were buried in those vaults.

"My mother's mother is buried there," Julie said, catching Jack staring at the cemetery.

"I know", Jack said. "I was with her during her Last

Rights."

Once the carriage was parked, we immediately entered the restaurant and found it a hectic buzz of energy. People were everywhere, idling by the maître d' stand, sitting or crowding the bar, walking to and fro. There were waiters, back waiters and food runners frantically working the room. Two bartenders danced around each other behind the bar as they mixed and poured drinks.

"Jzoo-lee, bienvenu!" Who iz zis wonderful looking man?" Francois said, smiling while standing behind his podium.

"This Francois, is my brother, Jack, Julie said as convincingly as possible.

"Brother, wei? Ah! Wei, I zee the family rezemblance!" he said with a satisfied look. "I am not so zure you mentioned a brother before, no?"

Julie was lost for just a second and quickly replied, "No Francois, I suppose I neglected to mention him. We've been estranged. He's recently back in my life and this is kind of a reunion."

"Fantastique! Right this way my dearest."

Francois led us through the menagerie of people to a beautiful outdoor patio setting and a fantastic table.

A polyglot, Francois was born in Paris but grew up in Munich. He had a French mother and a German father. He earned a masters degree in hospitality from Cornell University and since then had built quite a reputation in the hospitality industry in New Orleans. He speaks fluent French, German and English. Giving him a very distinct accent. He hammed up the French while on the job but could never quite get rid of the German underpinnings.

The weather had turned colder, but several outdoor heaters were enough to take the chill out of the air. Francois handed us our menus and informed us our waiter would take our order but he would like to start us off with a couple alcoholic beverages. I ordered a Highland Park 18-Year-Old and Julie ordered a Cosmo with Grey Goose Le Citron'. He and Julie gabbed on for about 5 minutes and then politely, Francois excused-himself. A back-waiter filled our water glasses and a waiter came by with our drinks and secured our order.

"I've always loved New Orleans in the fall," Jack said casually.

"Yes, spring is nice, but I agree with you that fall is far more rewarding. That lion of heat and humidity is tamed and we are left with a rather pleasant little kitty cat," Julie said and laughed at her own joke.
The two continued to chat idly until a food runner came and delivered their appetizers. Jack ordered boudin and smoked ponce. Julie ordered shrimp and Tasso Henican. A bottle of Chenin Blanc was presented and uncorked by the sommelier at the table, compliments of Francois. ~

Jack continued his narrative on Jamaica from the time period of 1713-1714.

"Edward, or Blackbeard and I went on for close to an hour while he smoked his tobacco from South Carolina. We spoke mostly of the ocean and sailing. He told me about his adventures, holding back some of the more illicit details for my sake only, he assured me. We ended the evening with the promise to stay in contact and a commitment to rendezvous soon. We said our goodbyes and Edward departed.

I sat on the terrace for at least 15 minutes, steeped in my own thoughts until I heard a rustling noise in the bushes to my right. Startled and curious, I decided to go take a look. It was probably just some big rodent or a wild boar, I assured myself. But upon investigation I was startled to see Juliette pop up out of the bush. It took me a moment to adjust my eyes on her. There was no moon that night and the only light available was from the oil burning torches illuminating the terrace.

"Juliette?" Jack asked bewilderedly. "For the love of Christ how long have you been spying?"

"I wasn't spying, I was waiting for the right moment to approach you and welcome you home," Juliette said nervously.

"Juliette, mi amor! My heart sings at the sight of you.
I've missed you my love, I've been looking for you all
day. Where on this God forsaken island have you been
hiding?"

"I thought it best for you and your family to reacquaint
before you and I did. I heard of your arrival early this
afternoon and have not been able to think of another
thing. I've missed you my love and I'm happy you're
home," Juliette said with tenderness as teardrops fell
down her cheeks.

"We need to proceed with caution! I've thought of a
million different reasons and excuses for us not to be
together. I can only think of one for us to be together,"
Jack said. "Love! I love you my dear and I know you
love me. That's all that matters. I thought over and over-

of what I was going to say to you, but that is all erased. All that matters is our love." Tears welled up in his eyes.

We made our way back up to the terrace. We talked until the sun rose. I told her of my time in London and my contributions to the medical science community. She told me of her time here on the island. Her decision to move to the abandoned house. How father was kind and helped her refurbish the place. She told me my mother spent some time with her while I was away and she really enjoyed her company. We spoke of anything and everything we could think of to fill the void that amounted to six years away from one another. I couldn't help but feel centered and grounded around her. I kissed her passionately. I didn't want the moment to end. We agreed to pretend that we were just friends, as this would allow us to spend time together without spies. Our secret rendezvous point was this beautiful-natural cave about a half a mile from the river. It was

our own private Jamaican paradise.

Jamaica,"Xaymaca" as it was called by earlier settlers, means "land of wood and water". It is a vast jungle of woods, waterfalls, rivers, creeks, estuaries, beaches, mountains, heat and humidity. Columbus first arrived in 1494 and the Spanish ruled until the English invaded in 1655. My father was a baron and mother was French royalty. They landed in the late summer of 1685. My father was granted land and built his plantation in a valley between the foothills south of the Blue Mountains and just north of what is now modern-day Kingston. Father dubbed the plantation, "New Essex." It was paradise. My only regret was not being able to spend more time there.

Juliette and I played our roles perfectly. We understood

the importance of keeping up the illusion. For the first

three months we casually danced around each other,

engaging only in quasi friendly conversation from time

to time. I even feigned interest in other women and

went out on a few dates but made it clear to Mother and

Father that I was primarily interested in learning

everything I could about the family business before I

wed. They were enthusiastic and supportive. They

appeared to appreciate my ability to maintain a

friendship with Juliette. Mother said friends like Juliette

are a once in a lifetime gift. She also mentioned that I

should never marry a friend.

Unbeknownst to my parents and hers, we continued to

meet secretly at our rendezvous point. We'd become

adept at slithering off in different directions and coming

together. Ultimately, I got tired of this charade and

asked for her hand in marriage. Juliette said- yes-

enthusiastically and we were married in the old way of

her religion. It was just God, his creatures, Juliette and I whispering our vows to each other and accepting one another in a lifelong union. Under the light of the first full moon of 1714, Juliette and I made love. We fell asleep naked in each other's arms. We woke up to the sun breaking through the leaves of the trees, got dressed and hastily made our way back to New Essex. To our delight we were unnoticed as we slyly went about our usual routines. Three and one half months had passed since that night, yet we kept up our ruse. One evening as Mother and I were having dinner, she casually brought up Juliette in conversation. Father was away on business.

"I noticed you and Juliette having lunch on the terrace," she said nonchalantly.

"Indeed, as you know we've maintained a rather pleasant friendship and on occasion get together and gossip about the island," I said as casually as possible.

"I did notice an extra serving; does she always eat like this?" Mother asked cunningly.

My heart skipped a beat and I hesitated but finally replied as best I could, "Apologies mother, I do not keep records of Juliette's gastronomic eccentricities. I will take note next time and ask her if she's well."

"Just curious!"

"What's that mother?"

"It's been brought to my attention that Juliette has been sneaking leftovers out of the kitchen. Chef has looked the other way but mentioned it to me in passing yesterday afternoon. Juliette is also favoring more relaxed fitting attire."

As Mother said this, I began to sweat. I knew I'd been ensnared. She was gifted at springing traps. It was her French aristocratic upbringing. Always a game of thrones.

I took a deep breath and said, "Mother, again my apologies, but I am at a loss, I-."

She cut me off and said,

"Jackson Tiberius Worthington, what in God's name have you done? You and Juliette have been spotted sneaking off the plantation into the woods at night on different occasions. I was praying your torrid love affair would fizzle out. You've courted other women before, but nothing materialized and now I know why. I allowed this flirtation to continue, only because I was certain that you'd get it out of your system. But that was foolish of me. Son, if you've impregnated the half-breed you've stained our family's house. It's been accepted for a long time that illegitimate children are an inevitability of plantation life.

"Bastards come after a man takes a real wife in the name of God. Your father has a bastard or two. We thought Juliette was his child until Ricardo fessed up to his affair with her mother who, in turn, denied ever having a relationship with your father. I would have allowed her to be your mistress but certainly not your wife. Well, it's not too late, I can fix-"

I interrupted and pleaded, "Mother please, it's impossible for me to lie to you. She is not illegitimate nor will our child be. Her mother and father were wed as she and I are. We've only recently discovered the pregnancy. This is a gift from God, Mother. A way for us to expand our family and to thrive. She's my soulmate! I love her with everything in my heart and she loves me equally. Please Mother, please don't separate us! She says you've been kind to her while I was away. Please be kind to her now." They both fell silent.

"Father will be home tomorrow, she said, ultimately, conveying neither pleasure nor disdain. "He corresponded and informed me to get you prepared for a trip to St. Domingue in his behalf. You are to sail there and conduct his business by helping to secure our future in sugar and coffee. We'll hold a family meeting on the matter of Juliette after you return."

Mother said this as coolly as was befitting her station. I bid her good-evening, departed to my room and fell upon my bed in complete despair.

Two days after Father returned

He and his men escorted me to Port Royal. I boarded our flagship vessel, a merchant-class cargo ship. Made completely of oak with an enlarged cargo area. She was slow- but steady and impressive. I headed to St. Domingue, which is modern day Haiti. Admittedly, my-thoughts were dominated by Juliette and when we arrived at our destination, I tried to conduct our family business in the very manner that Father would. We negotiated our terms on coffee and sugar and settled upon what I was certain was a fair exchange. I spent the next several days learning techniques for harvesting both products. I returned home about a week later.

I couldn't wait to get back to the plantation and may have ridden the men on board ship a bit hard. They did not protest but glanced in my direction disapprovingly from time to time. I think some of them knew my secret. When I got home, Mother and Father were waiting for me in the parlor. I entered and sat in a high-back chair after greeting them.

Mother sat still and Father fidgeted. I knew he knew. I knew he knew that I knew he knew. It didn't make matters easier for the two of us.

Suddenly, in a booming voice he said, "Jackson, what you have done son, has jeopardized the reputation of the Worthingtons and everything we've accomplished on this island. I'm proud of you for your scholastic achievements and all the wonderful contributions you've made since you returned. You've set more bones and sewed up more of our injured than I thought was possible. Your uncanny intelligence and insight of business matters rivals mine alone. We've raised you as best we could and thought you shared our values. Son, the world you live in will not accept this abomination."

Again, silence prevailed. No one moved a muscle.

"I've sold the girl to Moreau. Before you protest, she's my property to do with as I please. I'm good to my slaves and treat them better than anyone on this island. Our pedigree demands purity and I cannot stand idly by and watch my beloved son taint his or our future. My decision has been made and we will speak no further of it. This I have said and you will obey!"

I was put in my place and felt completely deflated by the situation. My father was a direct representative of the crown and his word was law. He'd never spoken to me like that before, nor did I ever hear him speak to another individual with such vehemence. He was beyond angry with me. He was incensed. I realized that there would be no negotiations. My heart was broken and I was deflated. All I wanted to do was run to-

Juliette, but that was impossible now. My mother looked at me with care and love in her eyes. Yet it was obvious that she accepted and approved of my father's every word, as she never interjected once on my behalf.

I held no grudge. They were my parents. They thought this was for my well-being as much as theirs. After several moments of deadly silence, Mother excused me and I darted up to my room, fell upon my pillow and cried harder than I'd ever cried before.

<u>**NOLA 2002.**</u>

As politely and tactfully as possible, a food runner interrupted their conversation with the placement of their entrees. Julie had ordered Crawfish Etouffee and a bowl of chicken, okra and Andouille Sausage Gumbo, both prepared Cajun style not Creole.

Jack went for Shrimp Creole and a cup of the Cajun Gumbo. There was an accompaniment of side dishes; Candied Smoked Bacon and Corn Maque Choux, Blue Point Crab Cakes and Catfish Fritters served with a House Romulaude. The side dishes were off menu and compliments of the chef via Francoise.

Jack had dined here on several occasions under Chef Paul Prudhomme and Emeril Lagasse. He was impressed with the balance of flavors, accuracy and execution by the kitchen and staff.

"Very well-orchestrated! Fantastic chef!" he said.

After the excitement of the bountiful feast settled in, Jack continued where he had left off.

Chapter Nine. Jamaica. 1714.

"I didn't leave my room for two full days. Father and Mother had food and water brought up by JoJo. A young house girl attended to my water basin and chamber pot. On the third day I cleaned myself up and decided to take matters into my own hands. I searched the plantation for my father, finding him in the stables grooming his horse."

"Father, I'm going to get Juliette back. Will you help me buy her back or do I have to go and fend for myself?"

"He simply laughed. He did not even have the dignity to argue with me on the topic. He then looked me up and down, turned away and walked off. That was the last time I saw him alive.

"I went back to my room. In my tall boy I had stored my rapier and two Queen Anne flintlock pistols my parents had gifted me one Christmas. I grabbed the powder horn, ram rod and lead balls. I wanted to make sure I had plenty of rounds so I laid out all the items on my bed, took stock and rolled them up in a sheet. I stored everything underneath my bed and waited for dusk. I had no real plan, except to storm Moreau's Castle in the cover of night.

I ate my dinner in my room and waited for the house to quiet down. It must have been roughly midnight when I gathered the sheet and its stockpile of armaments from under my bed.

"As quietly as possible, I snuck out of the house, made my way to the stables, saddled my horse and rode hard in a southwesterly direction towards Moreau's plantation. The light of the moon made travel fairly easy. I had been there a couple times before as a child but barely remembered the layout of the property. I still had no concrete plan of action, except that I would break in through the front door, and if anybody got in my way, God help em'! It was roughly 3:00 a.m. when I arrived.

"Jean Pierre Moreau was a 300-pound, 5 foot 3 inch cold- hearted lunatic Frenchman from Lyon. His family's wealth was secured in the silk trade during the late Renaissance. He built his plantation two years before my father arrived and had developed a reputation of mistreatment and abuse toward his slaves. He forced them to labor from an hour before dawn till an hour after dusk, 6 days a week. Only resting on the Sabbath due to social pressures from his religious colleagues and counterparts. The only break a poor slave had was passing out in the heat and when this happened they were usually punished or docked food rations for lack of productivity.

"He bought his slaves as cheaply as possible and in bulk. An average life expectancy from arrival to burial on his plantation was five and a half years. Kids who were born on the island were forced into labor at 7 years of age and some never saw their 10th birthday.

"I tied my horse up to a tree alongside a small babbling creek, giving it enough room to drink and refresh itself. I rode him hard without warming him up or cooling him down and I could see the stress in his eyes. The creature looked right at me, making eye contact. He neighed, stomped his left hoof on the ground in protest and looked away.

"Leaving the horse I walked the perimeter of the property in hopes of obtaining good reconnaissance. There were two guards standing by the front gate under dimly lit torches. They appeared entirely bored and half asleep. Moreau had enemies far and wide and I was sure that there were more guards patrolling the inside, keeping tabs on the slaves.

"I powdered and loaded my two pistols. Both now cocked and ready for action. I balanced my rapier in my right hand and then sheathed the blade in my corset. It was a gift from the Duke of Essex. Small, thin, sharp and light as a feather. So well forged and constructed that I could balance it on my pinky. Satisfied with my armament and confident in my mission, I made my way to the front gate as swiftly and quietly as possible.

"Gentleman, I'm here to see Moreau. He's in possession of someone who doesn't belong to him and I aim to see her returned." I said this with the manliest, deepest, most assertive voice I could project. Taken aback, the two guards stood at attention. Looked me up and down for several moments and then the guard to my left replied,

"Boy, the sun has not even risen, yet here you are startling us with proclamations and demands that are obviously above your station. There is nothing you can accomplish here and my suggestion and advice is to head back the way you came before we bend you over and spank you like the spoiled little whelp you are." Both guards chuckled.

"I demand entry and my wife returned immediately. I shall not ask again!" I shouted.

"Laughing almost hysterically now, guard No.1 looked at guard No. 2 and before he could draw his sword I drew my rapier and ran it straight through No.1's gut. After which I quickly shoved my right shoulder square into the chest of guard No. 2, knocking the wind out of him and throwing him off balance. I pulled my rapier from guard No.1's gut, turned on guard No. 2, elevated my weapon and then heard a loud explosion followed by an unbelievable amount of heat and pain in my left shoulder.

"Guard No.1 shot me in the back left shoulder. I flew forward and fell onto my stomach in the cold wet grass. My rapier fell from my right hand and my left arm was useless. I pushed myself up onto my knees as fast as I could, retrieved one of my pistols and fired dead center at the face of guard No.1, blowing a hole through the bridge of his nose and out the back of his head, obliterating most of his facial features.

"Gray brain matter, bone, gore and blood splashed all over the front gate. I dropped the first pistol and with lightning speed retrieved my second and fired into the chest of guard No. 2 as he gasped for air. I could see his exposed innards. Blood and gore were gushing out of both guards. I hadn't noticed before but guard No. 2 had slipped a dagger out and managed to stab me in my liver. I pulled the blade out and saw dark colored blood pouring from the wound. Accepting the-inevitability of my demise, I had only two choices. Free my wife or die trying. The latter being nearly accomplished.

"I gathered what strength I had left, rummaged through guard No.1's pocket, found the key to the front gate and unlocked it. I entered the compound and slowly made my way toward the main house. I was aware of eyes staring at me from the shadows. I heard a young voice whisper a warning that there were two more guards headed my way. My only defense was my rapier and a pistol I procured from guard No. 2.

"I heard the hustle and bustle of the two other guards running my way and realized doom was coming. The first of the two guards approached and yelled for me to halt, whereupon I leveled the pistol and shot him in his right shoulder. The man went down and the second of the two was upon me and ran me through with his sword damaging even more organs but thankfully missing my spine. I fell to my knees and the second guard raised his pistol towards my head. I heard a loud shot and thought I must have been hit again. But to my amazement I felt nothing and saw the guard directly in front of me, who'd held the pistol, fall forward face-down, a fountain of blood spewing from his back. He was shot by a young black slave girl.

"It was she who'd warned me of their arrival on the scene, stayed in the shadows and retrieved the pistol from the first fallen guard. With an old rusty kitchen knife, she managed to stab him in the back and pierce his heart. She then shot the second guard before he had a chance to shoot me.

"I was on my knees unable to stand when suddenly a man's strong hands picked me up, threw my right arm over his muscular shoulder and helped me to my feet. Half dead, confused and angry, I fought at first and then heard that same soft little voice tell me he's a friend by the name of Big Oak. She also told me he is deaf and speechless, but is a kind soul and wants only to help. I finally accepted the man's embrace and allowed myself to rest. Fatigue overwhelmed me and I nodded off in his arms for a moment before waking back up to the young girl's voice.

"Yoo 'ear fo' the light skin gurl?" she asked nervously. "She got yo baby, 'uh? She in da Mast'a house. He been betten 'er silly and makes to break 'er! She got pow-pow, we's a feel it mon. She be mo than slave gurl and he be knowing it mon! Big Oak' and me, we show yoo where she at. She'n 'is room."

"The little slave girl looked at Big Oak and pantomimed various gestures and mouthed several words that he lip read. It went like this: 'Fiyah deh a muss-muss tail, in tink a cool breeze!' Meaning there is a fire blowing at the tail of the mouse, but he believes he is feeling the effects of a cooling breeze.

"Suh! I's 'elp yoo wit' the bleeding. Yoo time to float the

river come and due. Be still mon'!" She wrapped her

scarf directly over my bleeding liver and guts and

cinched it as tight as possible. She also gave me a

drink with a pleasant almond-like taste.

"Opium! I felt warmth crawl over my body. A portion of

my life force was returning. I no longer needed Big

Oak's assistance, so he gently released me from his

embrace. The bleeding momentarily stopped, but I still

felt depleted of all energy. No movement in my left arm.

Yet I was able to hold my rapier in my right.

"I hep' best I can mon, time we go!" The young slave

girl and Big Oak escorted me to the main house and

through the front door. As we approached his bedroom,

I tensed up at the site of another guard. The young girl

barked orders and persuaded the guard to turn down-the hall and depart in the opposite direction from which we had just come.

"She looked at me with a smile from ear to ear and said, 'Him hates the fat mon moor tin yoo, me tink!' I tried to thank her, but she silenced me. Then she and Big Oak retreated in the direction of the last guard.

"I wasn't capable of busting the door down and running in to save my lady love like the gallant hero I'd pictured in my mind. But I did manage to open it slightly with the ball of my foot and push it far enough with my right hand to gain entrance.

"The fat man and Juliette were both in the room. Juliette on the bed cowering under the covers, naked. The fat man in a robe waddling toward a desk. The room was dark, yet I could see black eyes, scratches and bruises on my beloved's face. Horrified and sickened, I focused all my angst on the fat man.

"You despicable loathsome swine! You murderous bottom feeding cockroach! You defiled my wife and I will run you through for that indiscretion!" I said with sheer venom.

"Indiscretion? You simple minded child! You sneak onto my plantation, break into my home and call me a despicable bottom feeder? You insignificant little tadpole! I can buy and sell anyone I wish and do anything with them I please. Maybe I should buy your parents and sell them into servitude. Your father is still-in debt to me. He can barely keep up with the fees let alone the principle. I purchased this half breed for a penny and a half. She's my property. Now depart my house immediately and we will keep this little matter from the authorities. I am willing to handle it solely with your family. Naturally, I will be raising the debt on your family's obligation to include the loss of my men and God knows what other atrocities you committed this morning. Leave at once or I will shoot you dead where you stand!"

"He made his way to the desk and was rummaging for what I assumed to be a pistol. At that instant, there was a loud bang that left my ears ringing and I couldn't believe what I saw. Moreau's head exploded! I learned later that Juliette had managed to get a hold of the fat man's gun after he'd gotten out of bed and donned his robe upon hearing the commotion I made breaking into-his house. She hid it under her pillow and was waiting for an opportune moment to blow him away, which was obviously now.

"I stood wobbling and started to lose my balance before using the hilt of my sword to prop me up. Juliette leaped over to me and embraced me in her bosom as I collapsed. I knew I was dying but that didn't matter. All that mattered was that she was free and I was here with her. We both cried tears of joy, then my vision began to fade. The last recollection I had was watching her slice her hand open with my rapier. Then I saw her blood pour over me as she spoke rapidly in tongues. I passed out and didn't regain consciousness until several weeks later.

"Juliette filled me in on what happened after I passed out. She said the young slave girl, Big Oak and the good guard had returned. The young girl helped Juliette clean up and get dressed. They wrapped my wounds in the fat man's silk sheets. The sun was rising and the three were preparing to make good our escape. Most of the plantation slaves had risen and come out of their hovels to witness the goings on in the aftermath of the slaughter. A young slave boy toting buckets of water from the creek discovered my horse and led it up to the plantation. After being groomed, watered and fed as quickly as possible, it was handed over to Juliette and a smaller pack mule was gifted. The mule was to be the cargo carrier. I was part of the cargo. The plantation-slaves loaded us up with food and water and bid us godspeed and farewell.

"The slave girl, whose name was Josephine told Juliette of the 'Maroons', free black people who'd escaped the tyranny of the Spanish during the English invasion and settled in and around the Blue Mountains, mostly in the interior and eastern parishes of the Island. They would welcome her with open arms considering her power, whereupon Josephine winked and Juliette blushed.

"You say to da' Black-Mon o Wo-Man yoo cee, 'Ebry dyay debble help teef; wan dyah Gad wi help watchman.' Meaning every day the devil helps the thief; one day God will help the watchman.

"Juliette told me later that we traveled at least 10 hours the first day and another 12 the next. We were so deep into the interior of the Blue Mountains she thought we were going in circles and would die out there alone, yet better than dying in the arms of that fat disgusting Frenchman. I was told she ran into a small hunting party and greeted them with the proverb Josephine had given us. We were welcomed and escorted to an interior village of free black men and women.

I drifted in and out of consciousness for weeks. I went from eating only broth, then added yogurt, then meat and vegetables and finally I was myself again, wounds healed and consciousness returned.

"Six months went by. Juliette and I became productive villagers. I worked hands-on with engineering projects and medical duties. Setting bones, sewing up cuts and healing bumps and bruises, in addition to sharing my-knowledge of modern day building practices and technologies.

Juliette was among her religious ilk and expanded her knowledge immensely.

"One day a young boy came running into the village with an important message. My mother had written a letter to me after learning of my whereabouts. She sent JoJo and a black scout Father had commissioned as a trapper.

"The letter stated that Father died in a duel with Ricardo over our disappearance and assumed Juliette and I were dead. Ricardo then fled the plantation and hadn't been seen since. I was wanted by British authorities for the murder of Moreau and his four men. She arranged for us to leave the island with the help of my cousin,-

Blackbeard. We were to meet him in Spanish Town in

three weeks. She'd meet up with us there.

Francois made his way tableside where he prepared, executed and elegantly served Bananas Foster Flambé. A perfect distraction from Jack's narrative. Julie was awestruck to the point of being nearly shell shocked by his story. Jack was focusing on the three-and-a-half-foot flame that Francois masterfully ignited. Served over vanilla ice cream and caramelized with fire, Bananas Foster was his favorite New Orleans dessert. Community brand coffee with two shots of Jameson and cream were also brought to the table. The two revelled in the decadence of their treats in silence. Julie allowed the story of her family's history to sink in and Jack felt relief at finally having an audience. He'd mentioned tidbits of it to various other relatives including his granddaughters over the centuries. His-closest and most trusted contemporaries knew of his condition and were usually accommodating. But Julie was the most receptive thus far.

Jack had written memoirs that chronicled the last 300-plus years of his life. His adventures with important historical figures throughout the centuries were almost beyond belief. Some had played small roles in the storyline while others became dear friends. He took note of everything. He cherished the memory of how Blackbeard smuggled him and his wife out of Jamaica and the time they spent sailing with the notorious pirate. He also wrote of the excitement of his daughter's birth onboard the Queen Anns' Revenge, a hijacked vessel that became the flagship of Blackbeard's armada.

By contrast, the pirate's death and the events that led up to and followed were some of his saddest memories. He was most proud of joining the Americans as a surgeon in their successful revolution against the British. He detailed his time as a spy for America in the Mexican Revolution and that of being a surgeon for the Union in the American Civil War. He later wrote about swearing off war. That was until Hitler rose to power in World War Two and he served as a surgeon with the US Army's 83rd Infantry Division. At first he kept his diary on parchment, because that was all that was available, then later on the type of paper we now know before digitally transferring his material to computer disks and DVDs, which he stored in a safe at his law firm in New Iberia. ~

"Why are you telling me all of this Jack?" Julie asked with interest, along with a healthy dose of skepticism.

"It's all unbelievable but I swear on my beloved Juliette's soul that it's true," said Jack. "My Juliette, out of love, placed a curse on me. Modern day science fiction dubs it Zombification. She did not have the heart to let me die on the floor of that horrible Frenchman's abode. She used blood magic. As a result, I'm not alive, nor dead for that matter. But I did die, momentarily at least. My heart stopped pumping and my brain activity ceased. She invoked the power via ceremony and ritual and pulled my energy up through the earth by virtue of creatures that have a direct relationship to God. Thus, I've been in a state of cellular decay followed by rejuvenation for almost 300 years. It- causes an odor because of the decay of my DNA, my skin, hair, nails and what not. I'm constantly rotting and being reborn.

My condition is getting worse and the signs of rot are
more prevalent than ever. Without makeup applications
my skin is gray under most light. My nails are yellow
and my teeth are all gone. I wear dentures. My hair is
also tinged green. It took quite an effort to appear
presentable this evening, but soon I'll have to clean and
scrub again in order not to offend. But I'm happy to be
home."

"By home, you mean the shop? I now realize you're
telling the truth and at one time I do believe it was your
home. You've orchestrated an incredibly elaborate
evening. I'd like to know the real reason you've told me
all this. You keep mentioning your condition, this
'Zombification' and the powerful Voodoo that I must
possess.

She took a moment to breathe, then announced, "I have a performance this evening at Preservation Hall. Let's say goodbye to Francois and take the carriage back to the Quarta'. You can tell me en route the real reason. First, I must admit, I'm plrasedt that you've come into my life. This is all incredibly overwhelming though, so bear with me if I seem to be a little standoffish. You'd think with my upbringing and running the shop that this is everyday life for me but it's not everyday life."

Jack settled the check and left a generous tip. They said their goodbyes to Francois and promised to join him and his partner, Christopher, for brunch on his terrace Sunday at their condo in the Garden District, as they were invited. They left the restaurant satiated, perhaps even a little tipsy and boarded the carriage. About halfway back to the French Quarter Julie looked-over at Jack and asked, "Well? Bottom line, what's your intention?"

Jack hesitated and then replied, "I am ready to pass on and be with my Juliette. I have so many memories. In my life I've seen and done more than 100 men combined. I'd like you to help lift this curse. It's too cumbersome to continue. The vast majority of my time has been spent hiding in the shadows under aliases and disguises. I've seen revolutions and wars come and go and so many die while vast amounts of land passed between kingdoms. I have had a hand in much of it, despicable and contemptible as it was. I've seen the Industrial Revolution change the very way of life on our planet and the digital age that's coming. I won't survive the digital age. I'll be hunted down and caged. There're photographs of me floating around in cyberspace and a society that would love to expose me. The digital age is going to continue to grow and computers and-computation will dictate the very fabric of our society

and how we interact with one another. I will not be able

to survive all of the surveillance and eavesdropping

devices coming. People will consume media at lightning

speed.

"I noticed you have a cell phone. It's currently analog

but will be digitized soon and then computerized. The

curse goes deeper than just my despair. Every

descendent since my Juliette and I had our daughter,

Josephine, has never been able to experience true

love. Only one child, always a girl, was born per

generation. This curse will be yours as well if you

cannot help me or will not help me. You have the

power, just like my Juliette. I feel you are actually

stronger than she was yet you have never had the

opportunity to learn your potential.

"Before Juliette passed into the next realm, she taught me the ritual that would lift the curse, but I was warned that only a relative in a future generation could perform it. Since the curse was created out of love, it can be lifted only by a loved one. I know the ritual. I have studied it assiduously over the centuries. I so much want to leave this world and you have the ability to help me be with my Juliette and break our family curse. Everything I've built is in your name awaiting your signature. You'll have full control of it all, including the law firm in New Iberia. I'm sad to say but lifting the curse will involve fresh blood, yours and mine. Blood magic! We'll have to visit Jamaica where I buried my Juliette next to the little natural cave by the creekside on our family's land. Please don't think I'm crazy. This is the truth. I love you, dear child, and I hope that your love for me is the same and we can bring peace to our bloodline."

Julie hesitated for a bit, then said,

"Come to my performance, stay over in the shop tonight and we will speak more about this tomorrow. Tonight, we make merry. We sing and dance and celebrate our ancestors!" She needed to get her mind off the immediacy of the situation.

Chapter Twelve, Preservation Hall. NOLA. 2002.

After arriving at Preservation Hall on St. Peter's they

quickly exited the carriage. Jack paid the driver

handsomely and bid him farewell. Julie retrieved her

compact from her clutch purse and powdered her nose.

The building was wedged tightly between two others on

St. Peter's Street in the French Quarter of New Orleans.

Flaunting a well-weathered patina, the building held on

to its original mystique. Age only added to the charm.

There was a second story balcony with a rusted

wrought iron railing guarding abnormally large windows

with the storm shutters closed. Various layers of paint-

that had flaked off through the years created a soft gray
patina on the storm shutters and facade. The antique
iron security gate with an opulent sunburst design was
perched above pointed rods juxtaposed below. A small
sign that simply said Preservation Hall hung from the
balcony perpendicular to the iron gate.

Preservation Hall supported the sui generis culture of
traditional jazz in New Orleans, which developed in the
local melting pot of African, Caribbean, and European
musical traditions at the turn of the 20th Century.
Preservation Hall was a rare place in the South where
racially-integrated bands and audiences shared music
together during the Jim Crow era.

Preservation Hall held no pretense. She needed neither
makeup nor disguise. Aliases be damned! Preservation
Hall was a testament to the ages. She cared not that
she was rotting from the inside out and the outside in.

Preservation Hall had the confidence and mystique of Jazz itself!

"I saw one of the original performances of the Preservation Hall Jazz Band here in 1963," Jack said as he walked back toward Julie. "In a stroke of genius, Allen Jaffe, founder of the band and a tuba player, toured the Midwest. Gaining an unbelievable amount of popularity and interest nationwide as well as overseas. The band has even played with the great clarinetist George Lewis, The Grateful Dead in San Francisco and a myriad of musical talent since. Besides the wear and tear this place has changed, not at all."

"I was invited to tour the East Coast with their ensemble but I didn't exactly have anybody to watch the shop. Hey, maybe since you're here. Oh, wait. Never mind. I forgot," she said with a trace of remorse.

Once inside the venue. Julie spotted her three-piece band, which included drums, a double bass and a piano.

She and Jack sauntered over to her band, whereupon she introduced him to the musicians.
Paul, the drummer was a tall lanky Irish fella from The Channel in his late 20s with black hair and hazel eyes. Solomon, who stood 5 feet, 10 inches, had broad shoulders, skin the color of milk chocolate, super long arms and long fingers, played the double bass. The pianist was a combination of several different ethnicities. His Asian features were predominant and he fancied Belushi sunglasses and a black Kangol hat. The man was obviously a fan of the Blues Brothers and Jack approved. They were all dressed to the nines in various black and white pieces of attire, while the bass player was adorned with a bright red bow tie.

I found a nice seat on a wooden bench in the front row as the musicians started their set. The inside of Preservation Hall is as worn as the outside. A treasure trove of memorabilia adorning the walls, including pictures and plaques, is priceless. If Preservation Hall closed its doors one day it could open the next as a museum.

The band struck up with a couple of traditional New Orleans Jazz standards honoring Louis Armstrong and other NOLA legends. To my delight they played a traditional Cajun waltz, "Jole Blon", and I couldn't help but get up and dance. The band finished the set with an Etta James arrangement, "I'm Alone Because I Love You." I was floored. She'd been a great companion of mine. One could even say that Etta and I had an on-and off-again love affair but mostly we maintained a wonderful friendship. She was one of a dozen people-who knew my family's history. I loved that woman and Julie sang her songs in a traditional style but with intonations and a zeal all her own.

"What an amazing set, you have chops young lady and your band's got skills! I loved y'all's rendition of, "Jole Blon!" Y'all jazzed up that waltz a bit I noticed but kept it in three-quarter time! Nice tip of the hat to Louie too. He'd approve. I will say when you started playing Sweet Etta James a flood of memories came back. She and I were friends, very close friends," Jack said to Julie excitedly.

After their 45-minute set, he extended his sincere compliments and placed several large bills in their tip jar as the band packed up to exit the stage. Julie respectfully hugged and kissed each musician in turn and off they went on their separate ways into the cool New Orleans evening.

Julie walked Jack back to the shop. They spoke mostly of music and Jack told Julie how he once visited Etta James after she retired and was living in Riverside California. They spent a few days together and that was the last time he saw her. Julie smiled with understanding and compassion and told him everybody deserves love, no matter what form and when. She mentioned to him that if she knew Juliette, that grandma would approve. At the end of the day, metaphorically speaking, Juliette knew that Jack would be coming home.

In Julie's own conscience, she was conflicted with what was asked of her. She wanted to help this man, this ancient relative of hers, this living relic and historical archive of the last 300-plus years of her family's history. He wanted to be with the love of his life, his soulmate and she didn't want to deny him that. She was also concerned for her own- sake. This family curse had to go! She knew what her answer was going to be but needed to sleep on it. This had been one of the most fantastic days of her young life. But she was tired and she needed to rest. They soon arrived at the shop.

"Thank you so much for the wonderful evening. May I call a taxi for you or possibly walk you to your place?" Jack asked Julie in a fatherly tone.

"No thank you! I would prefer the short walk by myself with my own thoughts. Besides I have my Gris-Gris around my neck and a very small antique Dillinger that grandma gave me in my clutch. I'll be by tomorrow morning at 10:00 to open the shop. Meanwhile, mi casa su casa.

Jack, I'm overjoyed but a bit over-amped by your appearance. You've come into my life and asked the world of me all in an evening.

"Allow me to digest everything and wake up fresh. I promise you I'll take this seriously. We'll talk tomorrow! I love you Grandpa, Great-Great-Great-Great Grandpa I mean," Julie said laughing while embracing Jack in a hug. Sadly she could smell a faint odor of decay through his fading perfumes and colognes.

Hugging Julie back, Jack replied, "It's a heavy burden I've laid upon your shoulders my child and I wish there was another way. I've asked enough of you this evening. I'm happy to be in your life, if only for a short time! I've known of you since birth and your mother's and mother's before and have encountered mostly pushback, skepticism or angst. Not all of them liked or had the presence of mind to accept me. You've embraced me and have been a wonderful audience and I love you for that! I love you Julie. Whatever decision you make, I will honor and respect your will and wishes and judge you not."

Fog crept in from the Mississippi and gave New Orleans a half lit smokey semi dark wet vibe. Even sound travels differently in the fog. They could hear faint laughter, cars and the sound of a fog horn calling out reassuringly in the distance.

Julie did a180 and departed in the direction of her mansion on St. Ann Street. Jack watched her leave and slowly fade into the dark of night. Then he retreated to the upstairs bedroom of the shop and started his customary routine of disrobing and cleansing. 45 minutes later he was flat on his back staring up, wondering what tomorrow would bring. He happily reminisced about the evening as sleep overcame him.

Standing in front of Cafe du Monde with a view toward Julie's shop, a shadowy man in a dark suit flicked his cigarette on the street and walked away as soon as the light went out in the upstair's apartment.

**Chapter Thirteen. NOLA. 2002**.

Awakening to the smell of fresh coffee, Jack was surprised to see someone sitting on the bed staring at him with soft green eyes. Confused and slightly delirious, it took him a moment to adjust to his surroundings. Upon recognition Jack smiled and greeted Julie, "Good morning dearest, that coffee smells delightful!"

"I stopped at Mother's and grabbed beignets and Community Coffee with cream. I'm sorry I startled you, I should have knocked," Julie said apologetically.

"Nonsense. I was dreaming. I was alarmed to see you. Sometimes it takes me a moment to adjust. I've woken up in so many different places I almost forgot I was here in New Orleans. I was dreaming of the ocean," Jack said, trying to ease her embarrassment.

"I'll leave you a cup of coffee and cream. Get yourself together and we'll have breakfast downstairs. I've got to open up the shop. Take your time. We don't close until 6:00." Julie smiled and quickly left the room, shutting the door behind her.

Jack got up out of bed, went to his chest and retrieved a set of Levi's, a blue button-down Oxford shirt from Calvin Klein and a pair of black and white Chucks. He combed out his hair, went through an abbreviated version of his morning cleansing routine and made his way downstairs.

"Good morning, Mr. Jack! Biegnets are in the parlor on the tray and if you want more coffee I'm afraid you're going to have to make that trip yourself," Julie said cheerfully.

"Thank you, I haven't had a beignet from Mother's Cafe in quite a long while, possibly a decade," Jack said, eyeing the tray.

"Jack, I gave it some serious thought last night and again on my jog this morning and yes, yes I will help you achieve your wants and needs but it saddens me." She couldn't bring herself to use the word "die".

"You so recently came into my own life and now you wish for me to help you get out of yours. Understandably of course, because you feel trapped. I am happy to be in a position to assist but truth be told-my heart breaks at the thought of it. If you say I have this ability, this power and you can acquaint me with the ritual for doing so, then it would be remiss of me to say no. It's a worthy endeavor, albeit a sad one for me," she exclaimed. "Yet, I'll help you Mr. Jack and I don't want you to think for a single minute that you have to pay me in return. I'll do it for the sake of doing it."

There was sadness in her tone.

"Your inheritance is yours alone," Jack exclaimed. "I thank you from the bottom of my heart! I've given you so much information in such a short period of time. I'm happy you've been receptive. I shall dwell on this no longer but with your permission I'll start making arrangements."

The two spent the remainder of the day organizing and cleaning the shop. Jack took a short walk and got back an hour before it was time for Julie to close for the day. They coordinated their thoughts over a couple of Shrimp Po' boys and Hurricanes Jack purchased while out.

The next day they met up with Francois and Christopher at their beautiful condo in the Garden District. Julie spoke candidly to the couple and revealed that she may have to leave town for a while but spared them the details. Christopher said he and Francoise would gladly take turns watching Julie's shop if and when it became necessary.

The next couple of weeks were spent planning and preparing. In her downtime Julie studied the ritual and memorized the words but more importantly the feel of the ceremony that would potentially lift the Zombie curse. If this was going to work it had to be out of love and she truly loved and respected this man for everything he'd done over the centuries to help her family. Still saddened by the whole affair though, she was in no hurry to see him off. Nonetheless, the day of the departure quickly arrived.

Julie woke up early that morning and jogged over to Mother's Cafe for the usual beignets and Community coffee. When she returned to the shop she found Jack in the parlor, dressed for travel. To her surprise, there were two men in dark suits arguing with him.

"Mr. Worthington, no harm will come to you or to Julie but you need to come with us peacefully. We have two agents out front on foot, another two in a sedan and one in the alley out back. We mean you no harm, we just have some questions," the tallest of the two said assertively to Jack.

"You're repeating yourself!" Jack replied coldly.

"You never mentioned who you are. What agency or society do you work for?" Jack asked.

"We don't exist! Not to the uninitiated, but you've known of our organization for a very long time. We almost had you in Berlin and before that Gettysburg but you eluded our capture, or so I was made to understand. An entire unit of our agency has devoted their career to studying your every move. We've copied, organized and stored away every photograph and tidbit of information on your escapades from Jamaica to England, back to the-

Colonies and repeat. You've stayed damn busy. And I must say, that for a man 310 years old, you still look like you did in your mid-20s. We know of your magic, "Voodoo" and the power you wield. If you don't come with us peacefully we will use force and if necessary harm will come to you.

"Probably wasted on you, here, but Julie is not as strong and is more vulnerable than you. The choice is yours. A few questions, a couple of days and you'll be back home and on your way to Jamaica as planned."

Julie, silent as a mouse initially while trying to absorb and process what she was seeing and hearing, finally spoke up, "And by all means who the hell do the two of you think you are? Some of my closest friends are NOLA PD. You have 5 seconds to get the fuck out of-my store or all hell will break loose! Jack, I thought you said this place was charmed?"

Jack looked at Julie with concern in his eyes and said, "It is, these men seem to know the charm's ability and have men placed outside of its circle. Their organization has been tracking me for a very long time and apparently has been watching you as well. I've stayed away from you for a long time in order to keep people like this at bay. Unfortunately though, they appear to have outsmarted me. I shouldn't have surfaced. It's been an amazing couple of weeks. If I don't go with them they will harm you! Don't worry, you can't keep a fox trapped that's smarter than you for very long. I promise I'll be back soon. I left you everything you'll need. All the documents and instructions on what to do. So you'll have to take care of matters before we go to Jamaica. The chest is yours. I'm leaving it to you so-that you may explore your talents. Be patient. Those-

realizations will come. Only you can access your gifts. I

love you. I'll be back very soon!" Jack had a tear floating

down his cheek as he hid the malice that raged behind

his vivid blue eyes.

Julie, dumbfounded and sidelined by the events,

couldn't help but cry. She didn't understand fully what

was going on but knew that she was outnumbered and

had to stand down. She realized too that Jack gave her

some necessary clues to resolve the dilemma. She

figured the most immediate play was to let Jack go with

these men. He'd been taking care of himself for over

300 years and she was confident that he would be back

as he said. If not, then sooner or later she'd go looking

for him.

Jack embraced Julie with a hug, kissed her on the cheek and promised to return soon. He was walking out with the two men when he got to the door, looked up at the silver bell and said, "As long as the bell rings the walls will sing and angels will have a place to rest their wings!" *The silver bell rang out in protest!*

Jack had been gone for nearly three weeks and Julie became rather distraught. He hadn't called, written a letter or even sent an email. She'd gone beyond grief. Lying on the floor wrapped up like a cacoon in a blanket, she stared at the chest trying to figure out a way to get it open. Try as she might, she wasn't able to get the darn thing to open. Jack said it was enchanted and stressed that it functioned best at her store. Jack told her the reason he built the store at that specific locale was because the Mississippi meandered dramatically in a switch back that created a vortex of power that could be sourced in perpetuity.

All in all, she thought she was going mad. Voodoo.

Magic. zombies and now secret societies kidnapping

ancient grandfathers. She was losing her faculties and

action was needed. She got up off the floor and hoped

to make it to the shower when all of a sudden, the chest

opened up and spit out what appeared to be a letter.

Upon further inspection that's exactly what it was.

Sealed in wax and not surprisingly it bore the

Worthington's family crest.

Julie broke the seal and removed the letter within, read

it and then reread it several times before she finally

accepted the full content and what she needed to do.

It wasn't going to be easy.

End of Book One.

Book Two: Grandma's Gris Gris.

Somewhere in the Atchafalaya Basin. 2002.

(Sample)

At first Jack was utterly confused and delirious. He

couldn't remember who or what he was. The only reality

was an overwhelming pain that ran from the tip of his

toes all the way to his scalp. His hair even hurt.

His eyelids fluttered and his eyes strained to take in the light of the room. He could feel heat from a nearby light source baking his face and barbecuing his body.

Just then a rush of adrenaline ran through Jack's body causing instantaneous awareness and cognizance of his surroundings. He'd been drugged, Stimulants!

Quickly he realized that he was hanging from the rafters by chains, stark naked and filthy. The smell of rot was so overwhelming he vomited bile and mucus down his front side.

Jack was in severe pain, combined with the shame he felt it was all he could do not to break down and lose his faculties. He assumed this was the outcome his captors were hoping for. He couldn't recall the last time he ate solid food. It was apparent to him that he had been-chained here for some time. His wrists were impossibly angled and most likely broken. His feet were bound together and hung several inches off the floor. He felt tubes and needles sticking out of various places all over his body. He prayed he didn't have a catheter or a colostomy bag shoved inside of him. He lacked feeling and movement in his hands and fingers. Try as he might, he just couldn't get them to move. What torture!

"Jack, you're awake! We were unsure if we were going to be able to resuscitate you this time. Although, it's not like you can actually be killed, is it?" said a man in a flatland American accent through a speaker hiding in the silhouette beyond the lantern that was literally cooking Jack.

"Jack, this can all end. The sodium pentothal injections and the methamphetamines are going to turn your insides into jambalaya. I'm impressed though, we were able to keep you awake for seven days, no food, very little water and you still possessed the will to fight our questions. 300-plus years of practice makes perfect. No bother, I'm up to the challenge, you'll either break or simply cease to exist, your choice.

Give us the key, the secret to your immortality, this zombification curse that your wife several hundred years ago placed upon you. You're starting to rot horrifically and the smell is absolutely unfucking real! My men refuse to tend to you without full contamination suits. You're disgusting! I've only been given 30 days to extract the information that I need from you before I move on to your family. In this case, Julie."

At the mention of Julie's name Jack violently thrashed around in his chains and swore oaths that he intended to keep.

"You lay one hand on Julie and I'll put a curse on you that will enable me to torture you for centuries. I'll break you down to the point of death just to rebuild you so I can kill you all over again. Neither you nor anyone you know has the power to be able to do what my Juliette has done…"

Jack was interrupted by the American voice in the speaker, "Jack, I was hired to gain information and intelligence on your abilities, because to date I have a 100% accuracy in collecting such information from prior commissions. My employer pays exceptionally well and I'll be damned if I'm not going to fulfill my end of the agreement. If I have to rip Julie apart piece by piece in-front of you I will. If I can't get the information I need from you I'm going to seal you in a concrete tomb and drop you into the deepest darkest recess of the Atchafalaya Basin where you'll sink to the bottom and be consumed by the sediment. You'll disintegrate to an inevitable nothingness.

The way that we understand it so far, the science behind your curse is that inevitably the rejuvenation will cease due to lack of personal hygiene while the rot and decay will continue to consume you until you're absolutely non-existent. You'll just be a forgotten memory, a disgusting time capsule of poor decisions and lack of foresight. No consciousness, no soul, just a blob of gelatinous scum entombed in a concrete prison and swallowed by the Atchafalaya."

A person in a full contamination suit entered with a black rod in his right hand and a curved knife about 6 inches long and serrated on the inside in his left and approached Jack. What he perceived was an electronic cattle prod and some kind of meat hook started crackling and sizzling at the end, emitting blue and white sparks.

Just then, the person stabbed Jack dead center in his sternum with the sizzling cattle prod, causing excruciating pain in his organs that pulsated through his extremities and ultimately fried his fingers and toes leaving the nails, cuticles and edges blackened. His singed hair only added to the cornucopia of pungent smells already assaulting his olfactory.

Jack was on the verge of passing out when the person

removed the cattle prod and then instantaneously

inserted the curved meat hook under his left rib cage,

causing a whole new level of immense pain. He

screamed out in agony and thrashed around like a

barracuda on the end of a fishing line.

To be continued…

www.ingramcontent.com/pod-product-compliance
Lightning Source LLC
Chambersburg PA
CBHW020540160726
47991CB00002B/518